MAMA ADJUA ꝰ
CHILDREN'S PHOTO BOOK

VEGETABLES IN ENGLISH AND TWI

To Eden,

from Mama Adjua
x.

MAMA ADJUA

🖤 🖤 🏴

Introduction

Akwaaba.

Welcome to Mama Adjua's Children's Photo Book of Vegetables in English & Twi.

I returned to London from Ghana in August 2020, after an extended six day trip which lasted 150 days due to the pandemic & decided to write this book.

During my stay I began learning a few words in Twi, one of the main languages spoken in Ghana. The official language is English & there are over 50 local languages spoken, which include Ga, Hausa, Ewe, Fante & Pidgin English.

Which language do you speak?

Ghana is one of 54 countries in the continent of Africa. It is found in West Africa, between Togo, Ivory Coast, Bukino Faso & the Atlantic Ocean.

Can you see Ghana on the map?

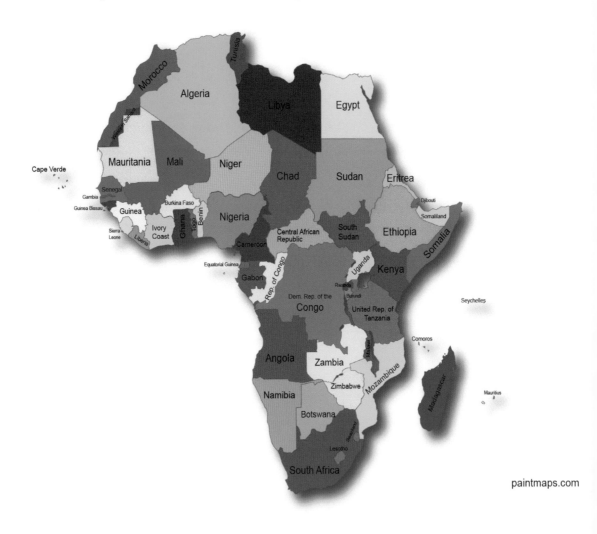

Join Mama Adjua & learn the names of vegetables found in Ghana, in English & Twi languages.

Do you know how corn (maize), okra or plantains grow?

I hope you enjoy learning & practising the words.

The book is available in Kindle & audio book from Amazon

Vegetables

Aubergine

Atropo

Ah-tro-poh

Beans

Ɛdua/Adua

Ed-we-ah

Beetroot

Ahwerew

Ah-sh-row

Bitter Melon

Nyanya

Ne-yah-ne-yah

Broccoli

Broccoli

Broc-coli

Butternut Squash

Ntɔmmɔ

Un-tom-mo

Cabbage

Kabegyi

Kab-age-gee

Carrot

Karɔte

Car-rot

Cassava

Bankye

Ban-chee

Cauliflower

Kɔliflawa

Cau-li-flower

Coco Yam

Mankani

Man-ken-ni

Coco Yam Leaves

Kontomire

Kon-tum-reh

Corn (Maize)

Aburo

Eh-bro

Garden Eggs

Nyaadewa

In-yah-doh-wah

Garlic

Galeke

Gar-le-ke

Ginger

Akekaduro

Ah-ke-kad-row

Lettuce

Mmrobo/lɛtuse

Let-tu-see

Mushrooms

Mmire

Em-ma-ray

Okra

Nkuruma

En-kroo-ma

Onion

Gyeene

Jay-nay

Palm Nut

Abε

Ah-beh

Pepper

Mako

Meh-ko

Plantain

Borɔdeɛ

Bro-dear

Potato

Aborɔfo mankani

Ah-bro-for man-ka-ni

Spinach

Srahansoe

Sah-an-swey

Sweet Potatoes

Atommo

Ah-tom-mo

Turkey Berries

Abeduro

Ah-bed-row

Yam

Bayerɛ

Bah-year-reh

About the Author

Mama Adjua is a Nurse, Health Visitor, Photographer & Author. She enjoys reading, writing, painting, upholstery, furniture renovation, dress making, baking & genealogy. She is a member of Kiwanis Club of Croydon, an International Charity supporting children & the founder of We-Stap, providing menstrual products & toiletries to clients in Croydon, London.

Mama Adjua is the author of The Overstayer, a collection of poems written during her six day trip to Ghana, which became 150 days due to the pandemic & lockdown. She is also the first UK Ghana Guru, promoting tourism in Ghana & encouraging people to visit.

Look out for her Children's Photo Book on Fruits in English & Twi, plus more in 2023!

The Overstayer Link

ISBN: 9798565288360

https://amzn.to/3UTJMIQ

Published by: Dr Ava Eagle Brown: business@avaeaglebrown.com

Photo Credits:

All photos taken by Mama Adjua except Mushrooms by Laila_585 Pixabay

Book Coach: Dr Ava Eagle Brown

Email: Business@avaeaglebrown.com

Contact Mama Adjua at:

- Hi@withlovefromghana.com
- www.withlovefromghana.com
- Insta @withlovefromghana

Printed in Great Britain
by Amazon

17874048R00022